Strange Ex

Robert Abernathy

Alpha Editions

This edition published in 2024

ISBN : 9789362994202

Design and Setting By
Alpha Editions
www.alphaedis.com
Email - info@alphaedis.com

As per information held with us this book is in Public Domain.
This book is a reproduction of an important historical work. Alpha Editions uses the best technology to reproduce historical work in the same manner it was first published to preserve its original nature. Any marks or number seen are left intentionally to preserve its true form.

STRANGE EXODUS

By ROBERT ABERNATHY

Gigantic, mindless, the Monsters had come out of interstellar space to devour Earth. They gnawed at her soil, drank deep of her seas. Where, on this gutted cosmic carcass, could humanity flee?

Westover got a shock when he stumbled onto the monster, for all that he knew one had been through here.

He had been following the high ground toward the hills, alternately splashing through waist-deep water and climbing onto comparatively dry knolls. To right and left of him was the sullen noise of the river in flood, and behind him, too, the rising water he had barely escaped. The night was overcast, the moon a faint disk of glow that left river and hills and even the mud underfoot invisible.

He had not sought in his mind for the flood's cause, but had merely taken it numbly as part of the fury and confusion of a world in ruin. Anyway, he was dead tired out on his feet.

He sensed more than saw the looming wall before him, but he thought it the bare ledge-rock of a stripped hillside until he stepped into a small pot-hole and lurched forward, and his outflung hands sank into the slime that covered a surface faintly, horrifyingly resilient.

He recoiled as if seared, and retreated, slithering in the muck. For moments his mind was full of dark formless panic; then he took a firm hold on himself and tried to comprehend the situation.

Nothing was distinguishable beyond a few yards, but his mind's eye could see the rest—the immense slug-like shape that extended in ponderous repose across the river valley, its head and tail spilling over the hills on either side, five miles apart. The beast was quiescent until morning—sleeping, if such things slept.

And that explained the flood; the monster's body had formed an unbreakable dam behind which the river had been steadily piling up in those first hours of night; if it did not move until dawn, the level would be far higher then.

Westover stood motionless in the blackness; how long, he did not know. He was hardly aware of the water that covered his feet, crept over his ankles, and swirled halfway to his knees. Only the emergence of the moon through a rift of the cloud blanket brought him awake; its dim light gleamed all around on a great sheet of water, unbroken save for scattered black hummocks—crests of knolls like that on which he stood, all soon to be hidden by the rising flood.

For a moment he knew despair. The way back was impassable, and the way ahead was blocked by the titanic enemy.

Then the impersonal will that had driven him implacably two days and nights without stopping came to his rescue. Westover plodded forward, pressed his shrinking body against the slimy, faintly warm surface of the monster's foot, and sought above him with upstretched hands—found holds, and began to climb with a strength he had not known was left in him.

The moonlight's fading again was merciful as he climbed the sheer, slippery face of the foot; but he could hear the wash and chuckle of the flood below. His tired brain told him treacherously: "I'm already asleep—this is a nightmare." Once, listening to that insidious voice, he slipped and for instants hung dizzily by his hands, and for some minutes after he had found a new foothold merely clung panting with pounding heart.

Some time after he had found courage to resume the climb, he dragged himself, gasping and quivering, to comparative safety on the broad shelf that marked the rim of the foot. Above him lay the great black steep that rose to the summit of the monster's humped back, a mountain to be climbed. Westover felt poignantly that his exhausted body could not make that ascent and face the long and dangerous descent beyond, which he had to make before dawn ... but not now ... not now....

He lay in a state between waking and dreaming, high on the monster's side; and it seemed that the colossal body moved, swelling and sighing—but he knew they did not breathe as backboned animals do. Westover had been one of the men who, in the days when humanity was still fighting, had accumulated quite a store of knowledge about the enemy— the enemy that was brainless and toolless, but that was simply too vast for human intelligence and weapons to defeat....

Westover no longer saw the murky moonlight, the far faint glitter of the flood or the slope of the living mountain. He saw, as he had seen from a circling jet plane, an immense tree of smoke that rose and expanded under the noonday sun, creamy white above and black and oily below, and beneath the black cloud something that writhed and flowed sluggishly in a cyclopean death agony.

That picture dissolved, and was replaced by the face of a man—one who might now be alive or dead, elsewhere in the chaos of a desolated planet. It was an ordinary face, roundish, spectacled, but etched now by tragedy; the voice that went with it was flat, unemotional, pedantic.

"There are so many of them, and we've destroyed so few— and to kill those few took our mightiest weapons. Examination of the ones that have been killed discloses the reason why ordinary projectiles and bombs and poisons are ineffective against them—apart, that is, from the chief reason of sheer size. The creatures are so loosely organized that a local injury hardly affects the whole. In a sense, each one of them is a single cell—like the slime molds, the Earthly life forms that most resemble them.

"That striking resemblance, together with the fact that they chose Earth to attack out of all the planets of the Solar System, shows they must have originated on a world much like this. But while on Earth the slime molds are the highest reticular organisms, and the dominant life is all multicellular, on the monsters' home world conditions must have favored unicellular growth. Probably as a result of this unspecialized structure, the monsters have attained their great size and perhaps for the same reason they have achieved what even intelligent cellular life so far hasn't—liberation from existence bound to one world's surface, the conquest of space. They accomplished it not by invention but by adaptation, as brainless life once crawled out of the sea to conquer the dry land.

"The monsters who have descended on Earth must represent the end result of a long evolution completed in space itself. They are evidently deep-space beings, able to propel themselves from planet to planet and from star to star in search of food, guided by instinct to suns and worlds like ours. Descending on such a planet, they move across its surface systematically ingesting all edible material—all life not mobile enough to avoid their march. They are like caterpillars that overrun a planet and strip it of its leaves, before moving on to the next.

"Man is a highly mobile species, so our direct casualties of this invasion have been very light and will continue to be. But when the monsters have finished with Earth, there will be no vegetation left for man's food, no houses, no cities, none of the fixed installations of civilization, and the end will be far more terrible than if we were all devoured by the monsters."

Westover awoke, feeling himself bathed by the cold sweat of nightmare—then he realized that a misty rain had wetted his face and sogged his clothes. That, and the sleep he had had, refreshed him and made his mind clearer than it had been for days, and he remembered that he could not sleep but had to go on, searching with a hope that would not die for some miraculously spared refuge where civilization and science might yet exist, where there would be the means to realize his idea for stopping the monsters.

He sat up, eyes searching the sky for a sign to tell him how long he had slept. Low on the western horizon he found the faint glow that told of the moon's setting; and in the east a stronger light was already struggling through the clouds and mist, becoming every moment less tenuous and illusory, more the bitter reality of the breaking day.

Even as Westover began frantically climbing, out of that lightening sky the hopelessness of his effort pressed down on him. With dawn the monster would begin to move, to crawl eastward impelled by the same dim phototropic urge which must guide these things out of the interstellar depths to Sun-type stars. All of them had crept endlessly eastward around the Earth, gutting the continents and churning the sea bottoms, and by now whatever was left of human civilization must be starving beyond the Arctic circle, or aboard ships at sea. The hordes that still lived and wandered over the once populous fertile lands, like this—would not live long.

For a man like Westover, who had been a scientist, it was not the prospect of death that was most crushing, but the death blow to his human pride, the star-storming pride of mind and will—defeated by sheer bulk and mindless hunger.

Near the crest of the monster's back, he stumbled and fell hands and knees on the shagreen-roughness of the skin; at first he thought only that an attack of dizziness had made him fall, then he realized that the surface beneath him had shifted. Unmistakably even in the misty dawn-light, the hills and valleys of the rugose back were changing shape, as the vast protoplasmic mass below crawled, flowed beneath its integument. In slow peristaltic motion the waves marched eastward, toward the monster's head.

He could stay where he was unharmed, of course. On the monster's back, of all places, he had nothing to fear from it or from others of its kind. But he knew with desperate clarity that by nightfall, when the beast became still once more, exhaustion and growing hunger would have made him unable to descend. As he lay where he had fallen, he felt that weakness creeping over him, no longer held in check by the will that had kept him doggedly plodding forward.

Again he lay half conscious, in a lethargy that unchecked must grow steadily deeper until death. Isolated thoughts floated through his head. It occurred to him that he was now ideally located to conduct the experiments necessary to prove his theory of how to destroy the monsters—if only someone had had the foresight to build a biological laboratory on the monster's back. Of course the rolling motion would create special problems of technique.... Idiocy.... Once more he seemed to glimpse Sutton's face, as the biologist calmly made that grisly report to the President's Committee on Extermination.... Sutton's prediction had been a hundred percent correct. The monsters' hunger knew no halt until they had absorbed into themselves all the organic material on the world which was their prey.... And men must starve, as he was starving now....

With a struggle Westover roused himself, first sitting up, then swaying to his feet, frowning with the effort to look sanely at the terrible inspiration that had come to him. The cloud blanket was breaking up, the sun already high, beating down on the naked moving plateau on which the man stood. The idea born in him seemed to stand that light, even to expand into hope.

Fingers shaking, he unhitched the light ax from his belt and began to hack with feverish industry at the monster's crusted hide.

The scaly, weathered epidermis seemed immeasurably thick. But at last he had chopped through it, reached the softer protoplasm beneath. Clawing and hewing in the hole he had made, he tore out heavy slabs of the monster's flesh.

A ripple that did not belong to the crawling motion ran over the thing's surface round about. Westover laughed wildly with a sudden sense of power. He, the insignificant human mite, had made the miles-long beast twitch like a flea-bitten dog.

The analogy was pat; like a flea, he had lodged on a larger animal and was about to nourish himself from it. The slabs of flesh he had cut off were gray and unappetizing, but he knew from the studies he had helped Sutton make that the monsters, extraterrestrial though they were, were in the basic chemistry of proteins, fats and carbohydrates one with man or the amoeba, and therefore might be—food.

His matches were dry in their water-proof case; he made a smoldering fire from the loose fibrous scale of the monster's back, and half an hour later was replete. Either the long fast, or involuntary revulsion, or perhaps merely the motion of the creature brought on nausea, but he fought it sternly back and succeeded in keeping his strange meal down. Then he was tormented by thirst. It was some time, though, before he could bring himself to drink the colorless fluid that had collected in the wound he had inflicted on the monster.

Thus began for him a weird existence—the life of a parasite, of a flea on a dog. The monster crawled by day and rested by night; strengthened, the man could have left it then, but somehow night after night he did not. It wasn't, he argued with himself sometimes in the days when he lay torpidly drowsing, lulled by the long sway, arms over his head to protect him from the sun's baking, merely that he was chained to the only source of food he knew in all the world—not just that he was developing a flea's psychology. He was a man and a scientist, and he was conducting an experiment.... His life on the monster's back was proving something, something of vast importance for man, the extinct animal—but for increasingly longer periods of time he could not remember what it was....

There came a morning, though, when he remembered.

Thus began for him a weird existence—the life of a parasite, of a flea on a dog.

He woke with the sun's warmth on his body and the realization of something amiss trickling through his head. It was a little while before he recognized the wrongness, and when he did he sat bolt upright.

The sun was already up, and the monster should have begun once more its steady, ravenous march to the east. But there was no motion; the great living expanse lay still around him. He wondered wildly if it was dead.

Presently, though, he felt a faint shuddering and lift beneath his feet, and heard far stifled mutterings and sighs.

Westover's mind was beginning to function again; it was as though the cessation of the rock and sway had exorcised the lethargy that had lain upon him. He knew now that he had been almost insane for the time he had passed here, touched by the madness that takes hermits and men lost in deserts or oceans. And his was a stranger solitude than any of those.

Now he listened strainingly to the portentous sounds of change in the monster's vitals, and in a flash of insight knew them for what they were. The scientists had found, in the burst bodies of the Titans that had been killed by atomic bombs, the answer to the riddle of these creatures' crossing of space: great vacuoles, pockets of gas that in the living animal could be under exceedingly high pressures, and that could be expelled to drive the monster in flight like a reaction engine. Rocket propulsion, of course, was nothing new to zoology; it was developed ages before man, by the squids and by those odd degenerate relatives of the vertebrates that are called tunicates because of their gaudy cellulose-plastic armor....

The monster on which Westover had been living as a parasite was generating gases within itself, preparing to leave the ravished Earth. That was the meaning of its gargantuan belly rumblings. And they meant further that he must finally leave it—now or never—or be borne aloft to die gasping in the stratosphere.

Hurriedly the man scrambled to the highest eminence of the back and stood looking about; and what he saw brought him to the brink of despair. For all around lay blue water, waves dancing and glinting in the fresh breeze; and sniffing the air he recognized the salt tang of the sea. While he slept the monster had crept beyond the coast line, and lay now in what to it was shallow water—fifty or a hundred fathoms. Back the way it had come, a headland was visible, mockingly, hopelessly distant.

Of course—the great beast would crawl into the sea, which would float its bloated bulk and enable it to accelerate and take flight. It would never have been able to lift itself into the air from the dry land.

He should have foreseen that and made his escape in time. Now that he had solved the problem of human survival.... But the bright ocean laughed at him, sparkling away wave beyond rolling wave, and beyond that blue headland could be only a land made desert, where men become beasts fought crazily over the last morsels of food. He had lost track of the days he had been on the monster's back, but the rape of Earth must be finished now. He had no doubt that the things would depart as they had come into the Solar System—in that close, seemingly one-willed swarm that Earth's astronomers had at first taken for a comet. If this one was leaving, the rest no doubt were too.

Westover sat for a space with head in hands, hearing the faint continuing murmurs from below. And he remembered the voices.

He had been hearing them again as he awoke—the distant muffled voices whose words he could not make out, not the small close ones that sometimes in the hot middays had spoken clearly in his ear and even called his name. The latter had to be, as he had vaguely accepted them even then, illusions—but the others—with his new clarity he was suddenly sure that they had been real.

And a wild, white light of hope blazed in him, and he flung himself flat on the rough surface, beat on it with bare fists and shouted: "Help! Here I am! Help!"

He paused to listen with fierce intentness, and heard nothing but the faint eructations deep inside the monster.

Then he sprang to his feet, gripping his hand-ax, and ran panting to the place where he had dug for food. His excavations tended to close and heal overnight; now he went to work with vicious strokes enlarging the latest one, hacking and tearing it deeper and deeper.

He was almost hidden in the cavity when a shadow fell across him from behind. He whirled, for there could be no shadows on the monster's back.

A man stood watching him calmly—an elderly man in rusty black clothing, leaning on a stick. The staff, the snowy beard, and something that smoldered behind the benign eyes, gave him the look of an ancient prophet.

"Who are you?" asked Westover, breathlessly but almost without surprise.

"I am the Preacher," the old man said. "The Lord hath sent me to save you. Arise, my son, and follow me."

Westover hesitated. "I'm not just imagining you?" he appealed. "Somebody else has really found the answer?"

The Preacher's brows knitted faintly, but then his look turned to benevolent understanding. "You have been alone too long here. Come with me—I will take you to the Doctor."

Westover was still not sure that the other was more than one of the powerful specters of childhood—the Preacher, the

Doctor, no doubt the Teacher next—risen to rob him of his last shreds of sanity. But he nodded in childlike obedience, and followed.

When, a few hundred yards nearer the monster's head, the other halted at a black rent in the rugose hide, the mouth of a burrow descending into utter blackness—Westover knew that both the Preacher and his own wild hope were real.

"Down here. Into the belly of Leviathan," said the old man solemnly, and Westover nodded this time with alacrity.

The crawling descent through the twisting, Stygian burrow had much that ought to belong to a journey into Hell.... More than that, no demonologist's imagination could have conceived without experiencing the sheer horror of the yielding beslimed walls that seemed every moment squeezing in to trap them unspeakably. The air was warm and rank with the familiar heavy sweetish odor of the monster's colorless blood....

Then, as he knew it must, a light glimmered ahead, the sinus widened, and Westover climbed to his feet and stood, weak-kneed still, staring at a chamber carved in the veritable belly of Leviathan. The floor underfoot was firm, as was the wall his shaking fingers tested. Dazzled, he saw tools leaning against the walls, spades, crowbars, axes, and a half-dozen people, men and women in rough grimy clothing, who stood watching him with lively interest.

The Preacher stood beside him, breathing hard and mopping his forehead. But he brushed aside the deferential offers of the others: "No—I will take him to the Doctor myself. All of you must hurry now to close the shaft."

There was another tunnel to be crawled through, but that one was firm-walled as the room they left behind. They emerged into a larger cavern, that like the first was lit—only now did the miracle of it obtrude itself in his dazed mind—by fluorescent tubes, and filled with equipment that gleamed glass and metal. Over an apparatus with many fluid-dripping trays, like an air-conditioning device, bent a lone man.

"Is it working?" inquired the Preacher.

"It's working," the other answered without looking up from the adjustment he was making. Bubbles were rising in the fluid that filled the trays, rising and bursting, rising and bursting with a curiously fascinating monotony. The subtly tense attitudes of the two initiates told Westover better than words that there was something hugely important in the success of whatever magic was producing those bubbles.

The thaumaturge straightened, wiping his hands on his trousers as he turned with a satisfied grin on his round, spectacled face—then both he and Westover froze in dumbfounded recognition.

Sutton was first to recover. He said quietly, "Welcome aboard the ark, Bill. You're just in time—I think we're about to hoist anchor." His quick eyes studied Westover's face, and he gestured toward a packing box against the wall opposite his apparatus. "Sit down. You've been through the mill."

"That's right," Westover sat down dizzily. "I've been aboard your ark for some time now, though. Only as an ectoparasite."

"It's high time you joined the endoparasites. Lucky you scratched around enough up there to create repercussions we could feel down here. You got the same idea, then?"

"I stumbled onto it," Westover admitted. "I was wandering across country—my plane crashed on the way back from that South American bug hunt dreamed up by somebody who'd been reading Wells' *War of the Worlds*. I think my pilot went nuts; you could see too much of the destruction from up there.... But I got out in one piece and started walking—

looking for some place with people and facilities that could try out my method of killing the monsters. I thought—I still think—I had a sure-fire way to do that—but I didn't realize then that it was too late to think of killing them off."

Sutton nodded thoughtfully. "It was too late—or too early, perhaps. We'll have to talk that over."

Westover finished the brief account of his coming to dwell on the monster's back. The other grinned happily.

"You began with the practice, where I worked out the theory first."

"I haven't got so far with the theory," said Westover, "but I think I've got the main outlines. Until the monsters came, man was a parasite on the face of the Earth. Fundamentally, parasitism—on the green plants and their by-products—was our way of life, as of all animals from the beginning. But the monsters absorbed into themselves all the plant food and even the organic material in the soil. So we have only one way out—to transfer our parasitism to the only remaining food source—the monsters themselves.

"The monsters almost defeated us, because of their two special adaptations of extreme size and ability to cross space. But man has always won the battle of adaptations before, because he could improvise new ones as the need arose. The greatest crisis humanity ever faced called for the most radical innovation in our way of life."

"Very well put," approved Sutton. "Except that you make it sound easy. By the time I'd worked it out like that, things were already in such a turmoil that putting it into effect was the devil's own job. About the only ones I could find to help me were the Preacher and his people. They have the faith that moves mountains, that has made this self-moving mountain inhabitable."

"It is inhabitable?" Westover's question reflected no doubt.

Sutton gestured at the bubbling device behind him. "That thing is making air now, which we're going to need when the monster's in space. It was when we were still trying to find a poison for the beasts that I hit on the catalyst that makes their blood give up its oxygen—that's its blood flowing through the filters. We've got an electric generator running by tapping the monster's internal gas pressure. There are problems left before we'll be fully self-sufficient here—but the monster is so much like us in fundamental makeup that its body contains all the elements human life needs too."

"Then," Westover glanced appreciatively around, "it looks like the main hazard is claustrophobia."

"Don't worry about a cave-in. We're surrounded by solid cystoid tissue. But," Sutton's voice took on a graver note, "there may be other psychological dangers. I don't think all our people—there are fifty-one, fifty-two of us now—realize yet that this colony isn't just a temporary expedient. Human history hasn't had such a turning-point since men first started chipping stone. Spengler's *Mensch als Raubtier*—if he ever existed—has to be replaced by the *Mensch als Schmarotzer*, and the adjustment may come hard. We've got to plan for the rest of our lives—and our children's and our children's children's—as parasites inside this monster and whatever others we can manage to—infect—when they're clustered again in space."

"For the future," put in the Preacher, who had watched benignly the biologists' reunion, "the Lord will provide, even as He did unto Jonah when he cried to Him out of the belly of the fish."

"Amen," agreed Sutton. But the gaze he fixed on Westover was oddly troubled. "Speaking of the future brings up the question of the idea you mentioned—your monster-killing scheme."

Westover flexed his hands involuntarily, like one who has been too long enforcedly idle. In terse eager sentences he outlined for Sutton the plan that had burned in him during his bitter wandering over the face of the ruined land. It would be very easy to accomplish from an endoparasite's point of vantage, merely by isolating from the creature's blood over a long period enough of some potent secretion—hormone, enzyme or the like—to kill when suddenly reintroduced into the system. "Originally I thought we could accomplish the same thing by synthesis—but this way will be simpler."

"Beautifully simple." Sutton smiled wryly. "So much so that I wish you'd never thought of it."

Westover stared. "Why?"

"Describing your plan, you sounded almost ready to put it into effect on the spot."

"No! Of course I realize—Well, I see what you mean—I think." Westover was crestfallen.

Sutton smiled faintly.

"I think you do, Bill. To survive, we've got to be *good* parasites. That means before all, for the coming generations, that we keep our numbers down. A good parasite doesn't destroy or even overtax its host. We don't want to follow the sorry example of such unsuccessful species as the bugs of bubonic plague or typhoid; we'll do better to model ourselves on the humble tapeworm.

"Your idea is dangerous for the same reason. The monsters probably spend thousands of years in interstellar space; during that time they'll be living exclusively on their fat—the fuel they stored on Earth, and so will we. We've got a whole new history of man ahead of us, under such changed conditions that we can't begin to predict what turns it may take. There's a very great danger that men will proliferate until they kill their hosts. But imagine a struggle for *Lebensraum* when all the living space there is is a few thousand monsters capable of supporting a very limited number of people each—with your method giving an easy way to destroy these little worlds our descendants will inhabit. It's too much dynamite to have around the house."

Westover bowed his head, but he had caught a curiously expectant glint in Sutton's eyes as he spoke. He thought, and his face lightened. "Suppose we work out a way to record my idea, one that can't be deciphered by anyone unintelligent enough to be likely to misuse it. A riddle for our descendants—who should have use for it some day."

At last Sutton smiled. "That's better. You've thought it through to the end, I see.... This phase of our history won't last forever. Eventually, the monsters will come to another planet not too unlike Earth, because it's on such worlds they prey. A tapeworm can cross the Sahara desert in the intestine of a camel—"

His voice was drowned in a vast hissing roar. An irresistible pressure distorted the walls of the chamber and scythed its occupants from their feet. Sutton staggered drunkenly almost erect, fought his way across the tilting floor to make sure of his precious apparatus. He turned back toward the others, bracing himself and shouting something; then, knowing his words lost in the thunder, gestured toward the Earth they were leaving, a half-regretful, half-triumphant farewell.

Milton Keynes UK
Ingram Content Group UK Ltd.
UKHW041820151124
451262UK00005B/700